LANCASHIRE FOLKTALES

LANCASHIRE FOLKTALES

A STORIED LANDSCAPE

JACQUELINE HARRIS

ILLUSTRATED BY
MARJAN WOUDA

STORYWHEEL

Published by Storywheel Press 2025

Lancaster, England

A catalogue record for this book is available from the British Library

ISBN: 978-1-9192344-0-3

"As for Jacqueline's own retellings: delight in their kick and terseness, their lyrical moments, their sense of mystery, their kindness"

- Kevin Crossley-Holland

To Sam and Sal, who are wonderfully grown-up now, but have shared this storytelling journey from the very beginning.

CONTENTS

Introduction   xi
Reference List   xix

KING OF THE CATS   1
South Lancashire

THE DUN COW OF PARLICK   7
Parlick Fell

ICY FINGERS   13
Garstang

LADY SYBIL AND THE MILK-WHITE DOE   19
Hapton and Cliviger

THE HEADLESS WOMAN   25
Longridge

THE JUG AND THE SIXPENCE   33
Thornton

PEG O' THE WELL   37
Clitheroe

SKRIKER   45
Chipping

THE TAILOR OF CHATBURN   49
Chatburn

THE WHITE DOBBIE   57
Bardsea

BURIED TREASURE   61
Salmesbury

THE BLACK COCKEREL   69
Lancashire

THE EARTHENWARE GOOSE   73
Singleton

THE ENCHANTED FISHERMAN   81
Morecambe Bay

THE SPECTRAL CAT   87
Leyland

THE EAGLE AND CHILD   95
Lathom Park

THE FAIRY WELL   101
Staining

THE LOP-EARED RABBIT   105
Crank

THE BOGGART'S HOLE   111
Blackley, Manchester

Notes and Sources   115
Bibliography   127
Acknowledgments   129
About the Author   131
About the Artist   133

INTRODUCTION
THE SECRET LIFE OF STORIES: NOTES ON HOW AND WHY WE TELL THEM

It's never only about the stories. It's about the nature of storytelling and story listening. After all, where is a story when it's not being told or heard?

As we criss-cross a landscape, there's an invisible layer of stories: local legends and folktales; supernatural tales that grow out of the relationship between people and place. They morph under the influence of new tellers and new times. They land differently in every listener, never fixed, always on the edge of their next becoming.

Professor Michael Wilson suggests that telling and listening are fundamentally the same activity:

"I would like to argue for the consideration of the view that telling and listening are not distinctly separate and discrete parts of the storytelling event and suggest instead that we might better understand storytelling processes and, therefore, the narrative cultures of which they are a part, by adopting a view that telling and listening are fundamentally the same activity and come together in an act of co-creation."[1]

It's been shown that a listener or a reader, fully engaged with a story, is in a light trance state. Their own imagination and the storyteller's words combine to create the tale that's unfolding in their mind's eye. The anthropologist Sue Greenwood refers to a state of expanded awareness that everyone has the potential to experience. She refers to this as 'Magical Consciousness'. She cites examples from shamanic and magical practices and experiences, but also points out that it can be experienced in many situations and contexts.

Storytelling scholar, Brian Sturm, has made a strong connection between light trance states and story listening. He gathered data through interviews and discovered that the experience of story listening had characteristics of trance-like phenomena. These include losing an awareness of our surroundings, experiencing a story as real when we 'lose ourselves' in it, changes in our perception of time passing, our senses fully engaged with the story world and being emotionally engaged with the story.

Sturm recounts how one member of a storytelling audience felt herself physically involved with the story, making involuntary movements that reflected the movements in the action of the story. Other audience members also found themselves identifying with the story in the first person. I once told a class of fourteen year olds a forty-five minute version of Bluebeard**. One of the boys (usually as talkative as myself!) had been completely silent for over twenty five minutes, eyes fixed on me. When we reached the part of the story where Bluebeard sees blood seeping out from underneath the bed, he shouted out spontaneously, "I'll save her!".

These characteristics are at the heart of how we engage with stories when we're fully immersed in them. They are the same as those that can be attributed to trance states associated with practices such as meditation, shamanic journeying, hypnosis and ritual. Magical Consciousness is part of our everyday lives.

There's an oft repeated maxim among modern storytellers that you should tell the stories 'that are yours to tell'. The stories I choose to tell are those that have meaning for me, those that have 'captured my imagination'. This capturing could be seen as the process by which I notice a resonance between something in the story I'm hearing and the stories I already know, both consciously and subconsciously.

By 'stories I already know', I'm including those I tell about my life, both to others and to myself. When we tell someone something about our lives, we're curating the information available to us and present it in the form of a narrative that, while having a relationship to reality, is not reality, but rather something closer to a photograph or a painting; a representation of something seen or felt. Drawing any definite line between reality and imagination when talking about story becomes problematic, because as soon as we talk about any experience, we're narrativising it. As soon as we do this, there's a gap created between the reality of what actually happened and the imagination we're now using to recreate that reality. Jack Zipes says:

> "We shall continue to use story in all walks of life, and the more conscious we become of how we use story, and why we do this to narrate our lives, the more we shall be able to cultivate honest speech in impossible times."[2]

Our lives and our stories are in constant dialogue: entangling, shifting, creating associations, resonances and responses. We're always in the midst of both.

Along with this recognition that we're always telling stories about our lives, both to ourselves and others, comes the realisation that the raw material for all fantastical stories is, and only can be, the experience of our collective lives. It's all we have. A dragon may not exist, but its colour is real, scales are real, fire is real: real life elements rearranged to create fantastical creatures. We could make up a story about a dragon that has scales of a never-before-seen colour, but we cannot, however hard we try, see that colour in our minds. All story is in direct relationship with our experience of life. The stories we hear only have currency for us if we see meaning for ourselves in them in some way. Our stories speak to each other, and we make meaning from the resonances we notice between them.

So what's really going on? I've come to see that we each hear the same tale differently. Through telling stories in different locations, including stages, schools, community centres, pubs, castles, gardens, recovery centres, stairwells and so many others, it has become clear that the place of the telling, the story about the event, the listeners own life stories and the thinking they're bringing to that moment are all part of what's happening. It all informs how a story lands, and explains why it will inevitably land differently in the mind of each audience member. A story will change again if we hear it at a different time and place. I'm not saying anything new here, we can check this out by remembering the feeling of reading a book or seeing a film for a second time, maybe years later, and experiencing it differently. The anthropologist, Tim Ingold, has this to say:

> "For stories do not, as a rule come with their meanings already attached, nor do they mean the same for different people. What they mean is rather something that listeners have to discover for themselves, by placing them in the

context of their own life histories. It may not be until long after a story has been told that its meaning is revealed."[3]

We can watch stories shift, change, mutate, rise, fall and change their meanings. The assumption that a story is a fixed entity, suggested by the phrase 'a story is passed on', begins to look flimsy. It has a done-and-dusted quality: job done. Rather, stories entwine themselves with a listener's thinking, mood, life and the existing stories that they bring with them, in a constant, never-ending process, with no beginning and no end.

The ubiquity of storytelling in our lives begs questions about who tells and who listens. There was a time when I contemplated creating small, immersive, theatrical storytelling events that could function in the same way as the traditional ceilidh: a 'house visit'. I'm using the word ceilidh in an earlier sense to the ceilidh we recognise today as an event that focuses solely on folk dancing and music. These house visits were rooted in communities and grew out of the people who lived there. Certain houses would be known as 'ceilidh houses'. Members of the community would gather for the shared entertainment of storytelling, music making, maybe dancing and games. I had even envisioned doing a tour where the venues were people's front rooms and the sharing of stories would be facilitated through a mix of planning and spontaneity. But the more I studied these traditional house visits, the more I understood that the meaning they held for a community came from a far deeper shared history than anything I could hope to engender as an outsider. A study of these visits has helped me to understand more about the complex relationships between story, people and place.

These ceilidhs are well documented in the social history of Scotland and Ireland. While there is little documentation of such gatherings in England, it is generally assumed that similar events will have played their part in the ongoing process of oral storytelling within rural communities.

While they offered entertainment on a dark night in the same way that television does today, this similarity overlooks what held these visits together. Because they developed from within the community. The content of the evening would arise from the relationships between the participants and their personal and shared histories. Connections between story, people and place would be constantly made and remade.

I recognise in this process the way urban legends function as they spread and are remade against the backdrops of different towns and places. When I tell urban legends in schools, the children, once they are privy to the wider history of these legends and how they travel, notice that a story told from the perspective of having happened just down the road has a very different effect on an audience than one that is said to have happened somewhere a long way away. There is a direct correlation between the perceived closeness of the story to the audience, and the sense of its immediate relevance to them. This often led to them excitedly reworking the urban legends to fit their own locality so that they could scare their unsuspecting friends; a process that has stood the test of time.

Thus, at ceilidhs, the supernatural stories would be rooted in the local landscape, offering a qualitatively different experience of engagement than a story with a generic or unknown setting. When listening to stories anchored to a particular landscape and told by the people who live there, you're located within the story rather than outside it. These stories are not separate from reality, but anchored deep within it. As the narratives lift off into the fantastic, the locality and the people are still right there at the centre of our imagining. We have a foot in

both worlds, the ghosts, sprites, dobbies and monstrous creatures coming to us rather than us to them.

As a listener brings their own knowledge of the landscape
to their felt experience of the story, so the landscape itself is
being storied for them.

The short film, "Gathered Voices of Lancashire" was a
collaboration between the film-maker Graham Kay and myself.
We wanted to offer a storytelling experience that tried to bring
together stories, their tellers, the backdrops to their tellings and
the contemporary landscapes that held them. The audience
would be the final part of the puzzle, each bringing their own
stories and life to their experience of the film.

The process began with the idea of collecting contemporary
supernatural stories first hand from across Lancashire before
deciding what form the final work would take. We shared
conversations and heard stories from people in pubs, cafes,
workplaces, hillsides, and anywhere else where people would
talk to us, following leads from one person to another and one
story to another.

I quickly realised that the stories we were hearing resonated
directly back to some of the old tales of Lancashire. Three of the
stories we gathered suggested to me three of the old stories. I
played with twisting them together, feeling for the moments in
the stories when they spoke to each other, using these to cut
from one to the other. We wanted to highlight how these
stories spoke to each other across time, with their roots firmly
in the same landscape.

It was decided that rather than directly illustrating the
stories visually in the film. The old stories would be juxtaposed
with imagery of the Lancashire landscape as it is now, including
locations mentioned in the tales, while the new stories would

show the tellers themselves in the places they were telling them.

Graham created his own visual language. This included some playful images that might trigger associations with the content of the stories. An image of two red painted discs on the old stone bridge appears during "Skriker": a huge shaggy black dog with "eyes of burning coals". A white dog on the beach at Bardsea appears on the screen during "The White Dobbie", a tale of a wandering ghostly figure and his scraggy white hare.

The stories in this book are rooted in the Lancashire landscape, their supernatural events and encounters happening against the backdrop of our everyday world. It's this that gives these tales their edge and bite. As you engage with these retellings, you become a participant in the storytelling, connecting, changing, working the magic of your imagination.

If the tales are retold, they become unique to the new teller. We are all the 'folk' of folklore. Right in the thick of it! When we encounter stories, we become part of their journey through time. They may be older than us and they may still be told when we're gone. New ones will emerge, but right now, they are of us. There's no tale going anywhere without tellers and listeners.

REFERENCE LIST

INTRODUCTION

1. Wilson, Michael. "Another Fine Mess", *Narrative Culture*, Vol. 1, No. 2, (Detroit: Wayne State University Press 2014) p 130
2. Zipes, Jack. "Foreward - The Possibility of Storytelling and Theatre in Impossible Times." *Storytelling and Theatre: Contemporary Professional Storytellers and Their Art.* Michael Wilson. (Basingstoke: Palgrave Macmillan, 2005) pp. xviii
3. Ingold, Tim, *Being Alive: Essays on Movement, Knowledge and Description* (Abingdon: Routledge, 2011) pp. 162

KING OF THE CATS
SOUTH LANCASHIRE

An elderly man sat quietly reading by the fire one evening when a cloud of soot fell into the fireplace and he heard a scrabbling in the chimney. He muttered to himself, "Those dratted birds," and pulled himself up. Before he was fully standing a huge wild grey cat landed in the hearth and leapt, knocking him back into the chair. It sat on his chest, prickling its feet against his jumper and searching his face. The man stared back into the cat's eyes; one amber and one green.

Then, the cat spoke. Yes, spoke! It said,

"Tell Dildrum that Doldrum is dead."

With that, it leapt back into the fireplace and vanished up the chimney. A minute later the man's wife came in. Their own cat ran in at her heels and settled itself down on the rug.

"What's that you've got on your jumper?" she asked. Looking down, the man saw two sooty paw marks.

"Well, my dear...this enormous grey cat...it came down the chimney, leapt onto me and said, *Tell Dildrum that Doldrum is dead!*"

His wife stared at him in disbelief, but their cat pricked up

his ears and jumped up. They both looked at him and he spoke.
Yes, spoke! He said,

"If Doldrum is dead, then I'm the King of the Cats!"
They watched as he turned and leapt up the chimney.

That evening, as the man and his wife searched the neighbourhood, Dildrum was taking his seat on a gilded throne, a golden crown on his head.

The old man stayed up late that night, staring into the fire until the last few coals glimmered among the ashes. As he stood up to go to bed, he heard a scratching and scrabbling coming from the chimney. Bending down, he watched as three starling feathers fell into the embers.

THE DUN COW OF PARLICK
PARLICK FELL

I n the village of Whittingham, on Halfpenny Lane, there is a house older than the rest. Embedded in its wall is an enormous rib from the giant Dun Cow that roamed the moors around Parlick and Bleasdale.

She would come every evening to drink at the spring known as Nick's Water Pot. People from the village would creep over the hill to watch her. She was larger than an elephant. If any of the villagers were in need they would bring a bucket or a jug and edge forward. The velvet coated cow would walk gently towards them, lower her soft black nose to greet them and turn sideways so that they could reach to milk her.

The villagers knew that she would fill only one vessel each. If someone was greedy and tried to fill two, she swished her tail. If they carried on she stamped her feet. If they still didn't stop she aimed a perfect kick and sent them and their milk flying. Then she would run away, disappearing into the mists and the night.

One evening, as the nights were getting long and an icy chill licked the air, an elderly woman sat at the window of her cottage, bent under a flickering light. She peered out over the fell and scowled. She knew all about the Dun Cow and how those fallen on hard times could take their fill. How dare it take away her business. At such times people came to her. They were her livelihood. A spell here, a lucky charm there and the outcome was always the same. When it worked, they were in thrall to her, and she knew what this meant: awe could be turned to fear, and that fear gave her power. She sat and stared at the glowing embers of the fire. Slowly she began to smile. Yes. She knew what to do.

The next night, she pulled her old threadbare coat around her, took a sieve down from its hook and hid it inside the folds of fabric. She left the house by the side door.

When she reached Parlick Fell, a straggle of villagers were heading out for Nick's Water Pot. She fell behind them and followed from a distance. Over the brow, she caught sight of the cow and smiled to herself. She dropped back and waited.

The Dun Cow was standing calmly as a young father with two young girls milked her. As the last villager passed heading back down the fell, she moved as swiftly as she could. As she approached the beast, she began to shuffle slowly, limping and groaning. Hearing her, the Dun Cow met her half way. She held out her arm. It shifted itself sideways and let her settle to milking. From beneath her ragged coat, she slid the sieve underneath its udders and began to milk.

She watched with satisfaction as the milk flowed straight through the sieve and onto the earth below. At first the cow was docile, but as the moon rose in the sky she became restless, swishing her tail. Still the cunning woman carried on until she had milked her dry. The beautiful great beast turned its head and stared at the milky rivulets pouring down the fell side; glistening in the moonlight. She looked mournfully at the old woman who stood back, held up her sieve for the Dun Cow to see and laughed.

The following week the father found the poor beast on the other side of the fell. She was lying as though asleep, but her soft wet nose was dry and cold.

ICY FINGERS
GARSTANG

It happened near Garstang in 1852. His name was Humphrey Dobson.

He'd spent an evening at the Frances Arms, sharing ghost stories. When he mounted his horse to ride home his friend, Jimmy, shouted, "Watch out for that Boggart o'the Brook!"

The night was still and the moon was bright, but as he approached the bridge over the brook, a tunnel of trees plunged him into shadows. At the very moment his horses hooves clipped the bridge stones, a high pitched shriek split the air. His horse leapt forward. He felt an icy arm glide around his waist and something cold lean into his back. He screamed. The arm around him tightened its grip.

His mare galloped on, her ears flat. With his last ounce of courage he put his hand down to try and loosen the creature's hold; and grasped a hand of bones. He tried to prise the fingers away but they were locked. There was a ripple of laughter by his left ear.

He glanced over his shoulder and saw a skull bleached by moonlight, shrouded in a billowing hood.

At the next corner, his mare stumbled. Humphrey was thrown sideways. He heard a crack, and then nothing.

When he came round, his head was throbbing. The sun was just coming up and his horse was grazing a few feet away. He lifted his hand to his temple and found his hair sticky with blood.

The next Friday he told Jimmy. Jimmy laughed and said it was the drink talking, but the man behind the bar caught Humphrey's eye,

"You're not the first to tell that story. A young woman was murdered down there a good few years ago. You're lucky your horse fell."

LADY SYBIL AND THE MILK-WHITE DOE
HAPTON AND CLIVIGER

Lord William of Hapton was in love with Lady Sybil of Bearnshaw Tower near Cliviger. She fascinated him with her clever and mysterious ways, but some said that she had heard about the witches at Pendle and wanted to be one herself, so that she could change shape and fly over Eagles' Crag with the curlews. He couldn't marry a witch.

Lady Sybil was in love with the wild open moorland that surrounded her home, and with a daily practice that involved the study of old books, long walks on the hills and quiet contemplation, she was indeed learning not only how to fly, but how to bend her world to suit herself and to help others. What Lord William didn't know was that she watched him when he wasn't looking, and kept her own counsel.

One morning, Lord William overheard one of his workers saying that they had seen Lady Sybil fly from her open bedroom window in the form of an owl, and that something should be done. Lord William decided he must rescue her from herself.

Everyone said Old Mother Helston, out on the moors road, was a witch, and thinking of the proverb, 'setting a thief to catch a thief', he set off to pay her a visit.

She was gathering mugwort in her garden when he arrived. When he shouted out she looked up and beckoned him in. He opened the gate. As she made her way to the door, he noticed she limped on her left leg.

She gestured for him to sit down by the stove, and said, "What if she doesn't want to be saved?"

Lord William opened his mouth but then closed it again. Instead he put his hand in his pocket and drew out a leather purse. When she saw the gold coins clatter on to the table she changed her tune. Lord William said,

"Please, help me to make her my wife."

Mother Helston looked at him steadily and said quietly,

"Very well, but she is stronger than you. All I can do is arrange the possibility. Whether or not she wishes to be your wife will be her decision."

He nodded slowly. Mother Helston turned away, bent to pick up a peat, threw it onto the fire and peered at the tiny flames. Neither of them spoke. It was some time later when she turned back and lifted her eyes to hold his.

"This is what you have to do. Go out hunting on All Hallow's Eve. When you find a white doe, throw a red silk cord around her neck and lead her to Hapton Tower. Make sure she's secured, then go to bed. Leave the rest to me."

On All Hallow's Eve, Lord William mounted his grey mare and set out with his hounds. He'd only been out half an hour when he saw her, a light and fleet milk white doe. He startled her and she fled. He spurred his horse after her, marvelling at her speed. When he got close he noticed a hound that was not his, keeping pace with her. He also saw that although its left hind leg faltered at each step, it was faster than any of his dogs.

This strange hound caught her by the leg. The doe tossed her head but didn't make a sound. Lord William rode alongside, took the red silk cord and threw it around her neck.The hound had gone.

He led her slowly back to Hapton and took her inside, across the hall, up the first wide flight of stairs and across to the small door that opened out onto the narrow stairs that led to the tower room. He led the way and she followed. He was amazed at how calm she was. He left the cord around her neck and locked her in for the night.

In the early hours of the morning a deafening crack and shattering had him sitting bolt upright. The curtains around his bedhead were billowing. One had ripped itself from the rails. He grabbed hold of it and held it back. The windows were unlatched, their black iron frames crashing back and forth as the glass shattered, catching the moonlight as it fell. His mind was racing now. A storm? For an instant the whole room shook. He grabbed hold of the bed posts. He must get to the white doe.

As he swung his legs sideways, the heavy wooden door flew open. Another wild wind rushed in, so strong it sent the heavy brass candlesticks on either side of the bed clattered to the floor.

He stood up. The wind whipped his legs with every step. The door to the tower room was wide open.

As he climbed the stairs, he noticed that although he could still hear the tempest raging downstairs, up here there was no wind, no crashing windows. He had expected to see an empty room. The white doe had gone, but there was someone sitting with their back to him in the centre of the room, outlined by the light of the full moon streaming in through the window. It was Lady Sybil, quietly combing her hair. She turned and looked at him. He had never seen such fearlessness in a woman's face. She took something from her lap and held it out to him. It was the red cord, now in shreds. He stared at it, his heart beating fast. He didn't dare to look at her directly now. He moved forward and took it, then stepped back. Lady Sybil stood up and walked past him to the stairs. He followed, keeping his distance. When she reached the landing, she raised her arms. The wind fell and there was silence.

Six months later they were married. Lady Sybil left Bearnshaw Hall to join Lord William at Hapton. The Tower Room was now her library and she held the only key.

Behind closed doors, her past was remembered and talked about in whispers. In public it was never mentioned. If it was, most said they believed she had left her old practices behind, but on a full moon some of them would watch as she left the confines of Hapton through the Tower window, silently taking flight in the form of an owl beneath the stars.

THE HEADLESS WOMAN
LONGRIDGE

It was late. Around the hearth in the White Bull at Longridge, Bill had insisted that his stories of ghosts and ghouls were true, but Gabriel was having none of it.

"You're mad, all of you. All talk. All talk. Too much talking. I'm off!"

He stood up and staggered to the door, stepped outside and took a deep, cold breath.

The quickest way home was through the woods and over the moor, where the track would lead him down to Thornley.

He moved swiftly through the trees, his mind full of the flittin' boggart, Peg O'the Well's ghost and the black cockerel sent by the devil himself. He tried to focus on the path in front of him, but when a branch caught his coat sleeve, he jumped as though Peg herself had reached out and grabbed his arm.

Soon he found himself on open moorland. As he walked, he looked up at the sky and for a few moments his thoughts lost their grip. He saw only the milky way arching over the heavens, the thickly clustered stars hanging like lace against an indigo sky. Then he caught a flicker of movement below.

There was a dark figure shuffling and shifting from side to

side about fifty yards ahead. Gabriel shivered, but as he looked he saw that it was only an old woman, swaddled in a thick shawl blanket and huge bonnet, carrying a large basket.

He ran to catch her up, shouting,

"It's okay, I'm from the village. My name's Gabriel. I'll carry your basket if you like? No knowing what ghosts and goblins might be about, eh?!"

She didn't answer, but held out the covered basket. He took it. A rasping voice said,

"Thank you. That's very kind."

But the odd thing was, the voice wasn't coming from the old lady. A screech of laughter made him turn. It seemed to be coming from the basket. He pulled off the cover. Inside was a human head, it's crinkled old face looking straight into his eyes. It grinned. Gabriel screamed and dropped the basket.

The head rolled out, matted hair and ghastly teeth chasing each other over and over. The old woman pushed passed him and stooped to pick it up. Her bonnet was empty. She had no head.

Gabriel began to run. Something flew past him. She'd thrown the head. It landed a few feet in front of him but he couldn't stop himself. He jumped, but it bounced up, it's teeth snapping at his ankles. It missed and he carried on running, the head rolling and jumping along behind him. He could hear it's gnashing teeth and shrieking laughter.

The track steepened. Loose rocks forced him to slow down, but the boggart's head was bouncing higher and further. It passed him and changed course, curving back into his path. Gabriel closed his eyes and leapt as high as he could. He landed safely beyond the rocks and raced to the bottom where the stream ran along the valley floor.

His Grandma had once told him that ghosts and boggarts don't like water. With that thought, he didn't head for the bridge, but waded in. The water was so cold his feet and legs went numb. On the other side he hobbled a few steps, looking back. The head was caught in the scrubby grass on the other side, it's eyes still looking straight at him. He heard a last cackle of laughter as he turned and picked up speed.

At home, damp and shaking, he collapsed into the chair by the fire and told his wife, Elizabeth, that he wouldn't be going out so much any more. She was curious, and prodded him to explain why. When he told her, she said,

"Well, stopping you from going out drinking is more than any woman with a head on her shoulders has ever been able to do."

THE JUG AND THE SIXPENCE
THORNTON

Margaret smiled as her favourite cow, Silky, lifted her head as she opened the gate. As she walked across the field, the other cows fell in line and followed her into the shippon. She tethered them, then sat beside Silky, breathing in the smell of hay and clover, and began to milk her.

The warm milk was streaming into the pail when she heard a tiny clink. Turning her head she saw a shiny silver sixpence on the floor a few feet away. Next to it sat a tiny cornflower blue jug. Clearly someone wanted milk. She took the jug and dipped it into the pail. Placing it back gently on the floor next to the sixpence, she turned back to Silky, closed her eyes tight and listened.

She heard a blackbird singing outside and the soft breathe and shuffling of the cows inside. After a few moments she half opened her eyes and turned her head. The jug had disappeared. The sixpence hadn't. Sixpence seemed a great deal to pay for such a little milk and she couldn't bring herself to take it.

The next day it was still there. Margaret leant into Silky's side and began milking. A few minutes later she heard the lightest 'clink'. There was the small blue jug and now there were two sixpences. She filled the jug, set it down and looked away. When she looked back a minute later, the jug had disappeared. She ran to the door, shielding her eyes from the sun and scanned the fields. The blackbird cocked his head, watching her from the hawthorn hedge. Back inside, she looked at the sixpences. Clearly they were meant for her. She stared at them for a few moments, then picked them up and dropped them into her apron pocket.

From then on, every day, she filled the jug and kept the sixpence. It was her secret. After a few weeks she threw away her old apron and bought a new one. A month later there was a new shawl around her shoulders. A few days after that Tom, the shepherd boy, caught up with her as she crossed the field.

"You're looking mighty fine these days. What's going on?" He grinned at her, "You got some fancy man buying you presents, eh?"

Margaret stopped and stared, her face reddening,

"How dare you?"

She glared at Tom, who looked rather sheepish now.

"I'm sorry. I only meant...well...that you look good..."

Margaret walked away, hiding her face, blushing for quite a different reason now. They were almost at the shippon.

She stopped.

"Alright, come in and I'll show you what happens. Sit next to me and Silky, and listen carefully."

They sat and listened, but there was no clink. Silky became restless. Margaret looked around. There was no jug. No sixpence. She buried her face in Silky's shoulder. The cow turned its head and nuzzled her arm, but it was no use.

She never saw the tiny blue jug and sixpence again, but some time later, the sixpences she had collected paid for her wedding to Tom, a beautiful cornflower blue jug and their very own cow.

PEG O' THE WELL
CLITHEROE

Mistress Starkie sat by her youngest son's bed. In the early hours he had one of his fits, tossing from side to side, his eyelids twitching. Now he had settled and she held his hand.

They had tried every doctor for fifty miles around and nothing had worked, but she knew whose fault this was. She was meant to be mistress in her own home, but everyone at Waddow Hall knew that the wooden statue of the ever young and beautiful Peg that stood near the spring by the river was the real mistress. Everything that went wrong there was her doing. Yet still she stood, mocking them all.

She knew why Peg was doing this: She was jealous of her because she was alive, made of flesh and bone and blood, while Peg, for all her power, was made of wood.

In the morning, when she left her son's bedside to call for milk and porridge, she had made a decision. She would send for the preacher who was known for his faith healing. It was time to fight Peg with her own tricks.

The next day she sat at the window, looking out for him. At three in the afternoon the wind dropped. Mistress Starkie watched as the pale cloudy sky took on a preternatural mauve tinge and fingers of grey blue mist fell low over the fields. She noticed the birds had stopped singing. Then the wind returned just as suddenly in sharp wild gusts, as if someone had flipped a lever. It sent weather vanes spinning, open doors slammed shut and the mist was whipped away. The sky grew darker, the clouds were a bruised glow of green and violet. The air felt charged as though something was about to happen. Someone screamed over by the river.

"Quick," cried Mistress Starkie, "Fetch help. It must be the preacher. He should have been here by now."

Fifteen minutes later, two of the servants carried the preacher into the kitchen. One of them dragged the sodden coat from his shoulders. They sat him down next to the range and brought blankets. His long dark hair straggled over his shoulders and he shook uncontrollably. Cook brought him a cup of hot ale with brandy and held it for him until the shivering stopped.

Mistress Starkie came in and pulled up a chair. She stared into his face. Her eyes narrowed,

"What happened?"

He took another gulp of ale and looked at her.

"I was at the Hipping stones at Brungerley...the river was calm...the stones were high out of the water."

He placed his hand on the side of the range to feel the warmth.

"I was half way over when a gust of wind hit and I almost fell. Then I heard it coming. The water was roaring when the wave hit me and my feet slithered off the stone. I was under... rolling through the water...managed to grab ...it was a tree root from the bank...That's where they found me."

Mistress Starkie stood up. It was Peg again. They said she

took a soul every seven years into the river, but not this time, and never again. She looked up.

"Fetch lanterns and an axe. NOW," she shouted.

A short while later, a small procession marched through the grounds, their coats billowing as they held on to their hats.

Peg's expression was calm and gentle as always. As they approached the statue, Mistress Starkie grabbed the axe from the gardener. Everyone stepped back as she swung the axe as high as she could. It crashed down, cleaving Peg's head in two. A second strike aimed at her neck sent the head rolling into the river. The wind shrieked and everyone stood silent as the head bobbed and spun in the water.

No one knows if the son was cured, but a spell was certainly broken that night. Now, there's no Peg to blame.

SKRIKER
CHIPPING

A storm was brewing as Peter left the Patten Arms in Chipping to walk home. As he entered the forest, the rain crashed through the trees. The wind in the branches whipped and cracked. He'd heard about Skriker. Peter thought if he could make it over the stream near Thornley, he'd be alright.

When he saw the bridge he considered turning back, but he'd come too far. He lowered his head against the storm and ran towards the bridge. He heard footsteps running alongside him. A great howl went up and he stopped, rain pouring down his neck. He knew it was there before he looked up. It was Skriker, a gigantic shaggy black dog Pitch black. As big as he was. Long legs and eyes blazing fire.

Peter walked forward. Skriker walked forward. He stopped. Skriker stopped. He broke into a run, fast, over the river, but Skriker was still at his side. He ran until he reached the front door of his house, but Skriker got there before him. In desperation, he raised his hand and hit out at it but his fist spun through air and struck the door. As he collapsed, he heard the creature pad away.

THE TAILOR OF CHATBURN
CHATBURN

"I'd sell my soul for a bag of gold."

These words were spoken by the Tailor of Chatburn. He had a long established business, a roof over his head and a wife that he loved, but it wasn't enough. Money came in and money went out, with hardly anything to spare. He found himself arguing with his wife over every little thing.

A few minutes after saying these words, he was stitching a sleeve into a jacket for the mayor and fell to thinking about his fight with his wife that morning. He could hear her in the rocking chair next door, rick, rock, rick, rock. Under his breath he said to no one in particular,

"I wish the devil would take her away."

But someone was listening.

There was a flash of purple flame by the door. The tailor dropped the jacket. A man with dark curly hair and a black fedora pulled low over one eye strode towards him. The tailor opened his mouth but his attention was taken by the quality and cut of the gentleman's long black frock coat, its lapels edged in velvet. He failed to see the small flick of a tail skirting the floor.

"How can I help you?"

His eyes widened as the gentleman's face broke into a sly grin.

"I can grant you any of those things you've been wishing for..."

That was when the tailor caught sight of the tail. He tried not to shake. He looked back defiantly,

"No doubt you would want something in return?"

"Only your soul, but I heard you say you'd be happy to give it. I'll wait for seven years before I take it."

There was silence for a few moments. The tailor took a deep breath,

"Can I have three wishes?"

The devil's grin widened.

"Of course you can."

"Oh, then a big beef steak! Right now, hot and pink!"

And there it was on the table in front of him. The devil watched as the tailor tucked in. Just as he was finishing, he said,

"Did I hear you say you wanted me to take your wife?"

The tailor nodded, his mouth full.

"I can do that for you!"

The last juice from the steak was dribbling down the tailor's chin. He wiped it with his hand and looked up just in time to watch the devil click his fingers. There was a cry and the sound of a chair falling over in the next room. He jumped up and ran in. Bess's chair was upturned, her knitting lay on the floor with half the stitches off the needle, and her shawl in a heap beside it.

"Done!" smiled the devil, folding his arms.

The tailor looked around wildly but Bess was gone. It was as though his whole world had shifted in an instant and fallen into a great black pit. He cried out,

"Bess, Bess, I'm so sorry. Of course I want you. Oh, I wish you were back."

He must have blinked, because there she was, knitting and rocking, as if nothing had happened.

He heard the devil's whisper behind him,

"See you in seven years."

He turned around. The devil had gone.

Over the next seven years he worked hard at his business. It began to do well. He became kind and thoughtful, appreciating every moment he had with Bess. There were hardly any fights now, and when there were, he knew better than to believe what they said in anger. They were happier than they'd ever been. Over the next seven years, he spent a lot of time wondering how he was going to outwit the devil when he came back.

Exactly seven years later, the tailor was about to close his workshop for the night. His hair had was almost white now and he stooped a little. He bent to pick up the key to lock up. When he looked up, there was the same black fedora and sly grin.

The tailor smiled ruefully,

"I was an easy catch for you."

"Yes. They don't come any easier."

"You didn't even get to show me how clever you really are did you?"

The devil frowned,

"Well no. There was no need."

The tailor frowned back,

"Well, maybe you're not really as clever as they say? It was easy to pick on the likes of me. Is that what you do? Only pick the weak ones?"

He saw wisps of smoke gather under the fedora. The tail twitched. The devil roared,

"Of course not! How dare you suggest...You should see me at my best!"

The tailor held firm,

"Well, then. Why don't you give me one last wish and I'll try and think of something really difficult for you."

The devil stared back. He stepped closer, his chest puffed out, towering over the tailor.

"Yes. You have it. What's your wish?"

The Tailor pretended to think. He walked to the window and pointed to a dun horse in the field outside. Then he looked back at the the devil and shouted as loudly as he could,

"I wish you were riding that horse back to hell, never to come here again".

A wild wind howled across the room.The tailor grabbed the table and held tight as it lifted the devil off his feet, carried him out of the door and threw him onto the horse, which set off at a gallop and leapt the stone wall.

Many years later, the tailor's house became an inn. It was called "Dule upon Dun" and the sign was painted with the devil holding on to the dun horse as it galloped away over Pendle Hill.

THE WHITE DOBBIE
BARDSEA

B ardsea doesn't get much snow, but in 1789, it was a foot
thick on the ground. Alice's sister, Mary, had come to
stay with her greyhound, Prince, in the tiny cottage
next to the church. It was a Friday night. Alice was in the back
making pancakes for supper and Mary had let Prince out for
a run.

After a few minutes, Mary opened the door and shouted,
"Prince, here boy!" There was a howl. Mary screamed. Alice ran
to the door and peered out, shivering in the icy air. There was
nothing there. She looked at her sister.

"I heard the White Dobbie," Mary whispered, "I saw the
white hare...it had eyes like hellfire and ragged ears. Then, I
heard his footsteps crunching on the snow... and Prince howled
and ran off on to the sands."

"Oh come on now Mary, that's just talk. I'll get you a
brandy."

The next night, Alice was called to ring the passing bell at
Bardsea church. It was a black night. There was no moon and

no stars. She only had a tiny lantern. The flickering shadows made it hard to see the rope. She found it and pulled. Once. Twice. Something white sprang across the tower. It was a white hare.

Then she saw him: The White Dobbie, in a large hood and rough cloak, a gaunt figure with hungry eyes. She heard his thin whisper,

"Who for this time?"

There was a bang as someone pushed open the church door. Alice saw the scraggy white hare with its bloodshot eyes leap inside the man's cape. Her lantern sputtered and went out.

"Are you okay? The bell stopped ringing."

It was Mary. Alice didn't answer. She could could still see him, a pale glow in the corner. She watched as he drifted towards the door, passed Mary, and out into the graveyard, where he melted into the shadows.

BURIED TREASURE

SALMESBURY

J ack and Will sat by the river throwing stones.

"You know Old Sykes and Mistress Sykes up at the farm?" said Jack. Will nodded. "Well, yesterday, when I went to take them some eggs, I got to the gate and I saw Mistress Sykes pulling the curtains. Then I saw Old Sykes go in and I heard him latch the door. I didn't like to knock, so I hung around and half an hour later they opened them all again. What do you think they were doing?"

"I dunno," said Will. Jack grabbed his arm,

"Let's go up again tomorrow and have a look around."

The next day they walked past Salmesbury Hall and up to the old farmhouse. The curtains were all drawn even though it was the middle of the afternoon.

"Come on," hissed Jack, "They must have left a chink somewhere."

They bent low and edged around the house. There was one patch of curtain over the kitchen window that had been darned one too many times and the fabric had frayed around the side of the mend. Jack cupped his eyes and pressed his face to the window. After a few minutes, Will said in a loud whisper,

"What's going on?"

Jack jumped down, his eyes wide.

"Well?"

Jack shook his head.

"I saw Old Sykes crawl under table and pull something out from underneath. Next thing there were gold coins pouring onto their laps. They were counting it and smiling. Then Mistress Sykes got down a broken old teapot from the top shelf. That was full of gold coins as well."

Will pulled Jack away from the window and pushed his face to the glass. Jack yanked him back.

"Stop it, they might hear us."

A few years later, the Civil War came to the north of England. Jack and Will hadn't thought about the Sykes for a long time. It was only when the old couple passed away within a few months of each other that Jack remembered what they'd seen. The farmhouse was emptied and searched but no gold was found.

Fifty years later the house was sold on to a young man called Edward. He was sitting in the garden late one afternoon, thinking how much he loved this old place, when he saw a movement over by the apple tree. He turned and saw an elderly lady in a long black wool dress with a large white collar.

He stood up and shouted,

"Hello. What do you want?"

She made no sign that she'd heard him. She was pointing

down at the tree roots. He looked down, puzzled. When he looked up again she'd gone.

Throughout the winter when he strolled in the garden at twilight, he often saw her, pointing at the roots of the apple tree. She never spoke and he never tried to speak to her.

It was early in the new year and Edward was sitting in the kitchen talking to a local man called Bill about mending the roof. They shared a whisky as the sun went down and he told Bill about the old lady. He thought he'd might laugh, but instead Bill frowned.

"You know, my dad used to tell me a story about an old couple who used to live here. Sykes they were called. Him and his mate had spied on them through a hole in the curtains, and saw them counting gold coins, but when they died, no one found the gold, but by then, it was the middle of the Civil War. If you ask me that was as good a reason as any to make sure your money was well hidden. Maybe they buried it..."

The two men looked at each other. "Shall I fetch a spade?" said Edward.

A few minutes later they were out digging around the tree roots. Soon, Bill hit something hard.

They unearthed twenty clay pots. When they opened them, the gold coins spilled out onto the grass.

Edward saw her first. He whispered,

"Bill, look. Look over there."

For the first time the old lady was looking at them and smiling. They both watched as she faded away into the soft winter twilight.

THE BLACK COCKEREL
LANCASHIRE

The huge black cockerel landed on the windowsill with a flurry of beating wings. It craned its neck towards the glass. Those inside were too busy telling each other tales of times past spent with the deceased, who lay in the coffin at the back of the room, to notice the watcher.

The bird adjusted its footing and looked straight at the coffin. At that moment a great crack of thunder came out of nowhere, so strong that the cups jumped and rattled on the tables. Everyone looked at each other. The father of the deceased raised his hand.

"Come on. It's time to go."

As the bearers carried the coffin through the door it lifted its wings and took off in what was more a leap than a flight. It landed on top of the coffin at the dead man's feet, puffed out its chest and raised its head.

"Hey," shouted one of the bearers. He took a swipe at the bird. The bird stepped sideways and then settled back where it was. The man at the other side had a crack with his fist but missed. Someone grabbed a branch and tried to knock it off, but a second later it was back, unruffled.

The father shook his head,

"We're going to be late. Let's be off."

The parson met them at the church gate.

When they told him what had happened he walked up to the coffin and grabbed hold of the cockerel. It didn't make a sound. Neither did it try to escape. He marched to the stream that ran at the bottom of the graveyard and held the cockerel's head under the water for quarter of an hour or more. There was a chill wind getting up and the small crowd rubbed their hands and shuffled from side to side to keep warm. A young man with a check scarf around his neck was the first to say it, in a whisper so that the father didn't hear,

"D'you think it's Old Nick, come for one of 'is own?"

Someone whispered back,

"Don't be daft."

The parson stood up, leaving the bird in the water. The moment he turned around, the bird lifted its head, stepped onto the bank and shook its feathers. Then it hopped back through the graves and stood on the coffin.

No one spoke. The parson tried to smile,

"Let's get on with it."

It was getting dark as they filled in the hole. The bird stood at the edge, never taking its eyes off the grave. As soon as the last shovel of earth fell, it jumped back on to the mound.

It was almost midnight when the father left. The huge black cockerel hadn't moved.

The next morning, the man in the check scarf walked past the church gate on his the way up to the farm. He stopped and looked over at the grave. The black cockerel had gone. He shook his head and muttered to himself,

"He's taken 'im then."

THE EARTHENWARE GOOSE
SINGLETON

Over the last month in Singleton, milk churns had been mysteriously emptied, milk had gone missing from the pantries, and now, this morning, it seemed that even the cows had no milk left in them. Some of the locals blamed the fairies, but Tom thought he knew better. Mag Shelton had been out and about a lot recently.

No one knew how old Mag was, only that she had lived in Singleton longer than any of them, in a rundown cottage on the edge of the village. She kept herself to herself, while her ginger cat sat on the gate and spat at passers by.

Tom jumped up onto the wall just outside the cowshed. As he remembered when he was seven, how he and his mate Jim had banged on her door shouting, "Ugly Old Witch". Jim had knocked her cat off the gate and they'd run off, but a few yards down the road Jim had collapsed. Tom had run back and got his dad. When they tried to help him up, he'd cried out,

"Someone should kill that Mag Shelton."

That was eight years ago. He jumped off the wall and set off down the lane to Jim's.

Jim was just leaving the house.

"Hey, I thought we were meeting up later?

"Tonight, you and I are going to Mag Shelton's. I've been thinking about her and it's time someone sorted her out once and for all."

They met close to Mag's cottage. Tom had brought a thick stick with him.

"Time we taught the old witch a lesson."

Jim looked around warily,

"Where's the cat?"

"It must be inside."

Tom pushed the gate. They lowered their heads as they made their way through the small garden, full of nettles, ragwort and rosemary. The kitchen window was only two feet off the ground. Jim peered in at the corner.

"Can you see any pitchers of milk?"

"No, but the cat's curled up on the rug. Wait, there's something else," he shifted himself a bit to the right. "Well, I've never seen that before."

"What?"

"She's got a goose in there."

"A goose? Inside the house?"

"Aye. Here she comes. She's picking up her shawl. Quick, get down the side of the house."

As they looked back around the corner, they saw the front door open. Mag shooed the cat and the goose out and followed them. She was hunched and walking slowly with a stick. Jim edged round the corner, holding Tom back.

"Is she carrying a jug or anything?"

"No, I can't see anything. No point facing her now, better to wait and see if she has any milk with her when she gets back. Then we'll catch her red-handed."

Mag walked towards the village, the cat and goose on either side of her.

It was past eleven when they heard the click of Mag's stick and there she was with the cat, coming round the corner. There was no sign of the goose. Tom whispered in Jim's ear,

"She must have the milk on her somewhere."

He stepped forward and lifted the stick. Jim pulled him back.

"Look, she's got one hand on her stick and the other at her side. She's not hiding anything".

As she reached the gate, Jim doffed his cap. Then the goose came around the corner. As it came closer, Tom lifted his stick. It came down on the goose's head. There was a crack and the sound of breaking china. Tom and Jim jumped back. Mag turned around.

The goose was no longer a goose, but a huge white china jug, now smashed to pieces. The milk was pouring into a puddle at their feet. Jim and Tom stared. Mag ran as best she could into her cottage and bolted the door behind her.

The door slamming roused Tom.

"We're coming in," he shouted.

"No", said Jim, grabbing his arm. "We'll be civilised and go tell the vicar what we've seen."

The vicar was locking up the church as they passed and they called him over. Tom was all for going straight back to the cottage there and then, but the vicar persuaded them to go home. It was agreed they would all decide what should be done in the morning. Neither of them noticed the vicar setting off up the lane as they walked away.

The morning came and the three of them arrived at the cottage, stepping around the broken china. Tom pushed ahead through the gate and banged hard on the door. It wasn't shut and it flew inwards. They went inside, but Mag and her cat were long gone. No one in Singleton ever saw them again.

THE ENCHANTED FISHERMAN
MORECAMBE BAY

Roger had been out fishing all day in his tiny blue boat on the bay. The sun was low in a pewter sky when he decided to call it a day. He turned towards home. As he slid gently through the water, a sea fret took hold. He could feel it's damp tendrils on his neck.

Then, out of the silence, a bell rang, deep and solemn. He grabbed the rudder and looked around, but it sounded as if it was coming from underneath the boat. He leant over the side and peered into the inky water. The ringing stopped, but when he looked up, everything had changed.

The sky was lit with a soft green light. The boat was gliding towards a coastline he'd never seen, lined with the gnarled roots of great oak trees that seemed to rise into the hazy sky. He tried to steer himself away, but his boat, with a mind of its own, carried him straight towards the shore.

It grounded on a small stoney beach. Slowly, Roger stepped out onto the pale stones that reflected a mossy twilight. A narrow track led deep into the trees. He heard something and stopped. Laughter? There was a flash of movement through the branches.

Out poured twenty or so small green creatures, each about two foot high, singing and laughing. When they saw him, they stopped. Six of them ran forward. Two seized Roger's hands while the others grabbed the bottom of his coat and trousers. Soon he was being pulled and dragged down the track through the now darkening woods. He tried to shout but nothing came out.

They stopped in front of a tall black granite rock face. One of them stepped forward and knocked. A hidden door swung inwards and they hauled him through.

A maze of passages led off in different directions. They turned left. Roger could see an orange glow. As they got closer he could hear fiddles and flutes. The passage opened into a great underground cavern lit by fire torches. Hundreds of the fey creatures were dancing, dressed in iridescent emerald dresses and cloaks. The red feathers in their caps flickered in the torch light as they swirled around. Children laughed as they were hoisted onto shoulders and swung between legs.

Roger's toes began to tap and his arms began to wave. Soon he was away, whirling as they pushed and caught him, guiding him across and around the dance floor. They wouldn't let go. He danced and danced, even as his head spun, his legs ached and his eyes closed.

Finally, he collapsed, and fell straight to sleep.

When he woke up, he found himself on a shallow green banking, split by foxgloves. His stomach grumbled. "I'm starving", he thought. There was a white flash and a plate piled with ham and bread appeared by his feet. He stared at it for a moment, then picked it up and ate. As he wiped his mouth, he caught a whisper of sapphire blue out of the corner of his eye.

He looked up . She was watching him. He knew exactly who she was. It was as though he had always known. She was the

Faery Queen, and in that moment he forgot his home, his wife and his children.

When she spoke, her voice was strong and clear.

"Do you like it here?"

Roger couldn't speak. He nodded.

She smiled.

"Would you like to stay here?"

He felt as though someone was pouring molten gold through his bones, and he nodded wildly.

She laughed as she turned and disappeared into the forest. He jumped up and ran after her, but saw only the white flash of her bare foot as it curved around a corner.

At the next bend, the path branched into two. He looked but she was gone. He slumped to the ground, his back against a tree. His stomach rumbled. "I'm still hungry," he thought. There was another flash. A white china plate filled with tiny wild strawberries lay on the ground in front of him.

As he ate, he found himself thinking, "If I can wish for food and it appears, maybe I can wish for gold?" The air in front of him began to shimmer and move, A pile of gold coins appeared at his feet, the top ones clinking and sliding to the ground, glistening amongst the leaves. He bent down and grabbed what he could, stuffing the coins into his pockets and down the sides of his boots.

He remembered his family and his cottage in Poulton. "I need to go home," he thought to himself, "I'm rich!" He stood up. Where was his boat? Facing the breeze, he thought he caught the tang of salt on his tongue and set off through the trees.

Before it reached the beach, the path opened out into a circle of trees. A group of the fae folk were gathered around something soft and white. Roger hid behind the nearest tree. He could see a pile of thistle seeds. He watched as they took one at a time, separating the strands and weaving them into the one before. They were making a thistledown blanket.

He looked up and there she was, on the other side of the circle, a young male fairy wafting her gently with a fan made of leaves and twigs.

Roger groaned. The feeling rose up from his feet and into his belly. It came out of his mouth as an anguished cry. He leapt forward and ran across the clearing, gold coins spilling out of his pockets. He lunged down to kiss her bare foot. The creatures pounced. They crushed him into the ground, punching, biting and scratching. Roger covered his face with his arms and shouted out,

"Stop! Stop!"

But they carried on until Roger wailed,

"Oh, I wish I was in my little blue boat on the bay."

Everything stopped. There was silence. Roger didn't move. After a few moments, he felt himself swaying gently from side to side. He took his hands away from his face and found himself curled up in the bottom of his boat, bobbing on a calm sea close to Poulton sands. He thrust his hands into his pockets and down his boots. The gold had gone.

In the days that followed, he told a few of his friends what had happened. Some believed him, some didn't. He never told his wife.

Over the months, he became restless. He stopped eating and when he wasn't out in his boat, he was often seen pacing over the sands or just standing, staring out across the bay.

One evening a year later, he didn't return from a fishing trip. The next morning, the tide was out. His friends found his boat upturned on the sands, but there was no sign of Roger. He was never seen again.

THE SPECTRAL CAT
LEYLAND

The foundations were laid. The stones were piled up in great mounds. All was ready for the next day's work. The vicar looked out over the field at Whittle-le-Woods and smiled to himself. The men had worked hard and the new church was taking shape right beneath his eyes. He yawned. It had been a long day.

Early the next morning, he pulled on his coat and hurried down the lane, wanting to see the beginnings of the new church in the soft pink glow of sunrise, but at the gate to the field he caught his breath and put his hand over his mouth. Everything had gone. No foundations, no stones, only buttercups and poppies leaning and nodding in the breeze.

He was still trying to gather his thoughts when he heard someone shout out. Turning, he saw a young lad running up, out of breath,

"Old...Adam's... well... cross with you," he puffed. "He says you shouldn't have... not without asking him!"

"Asking him what?" said the vicar.

The young lad shook his head, frowning.

"You'd better come and see."

The boy took the vicar straight to a field behind Adam's bakery in Leyland and pointed. The vicar grabbed the gatepost to steady himself. There were the foundations, laid out, and the stone, in Adam's field.

"What's this all about?"

It was Adam, stamping up the track. The vicar held up his hands,

"Adam, this has nothing to do with me."

"Who then?"

The vicar took a couple of unsteady steps further into the field and was silent for a few moments.

I'm thinking it's the old fella himself."

For a few moments no-one spoke.

"You mean ...?"

"Ay Adam, I do, the devil himself."

The vicar turned around,

"And we're going to undo all his hard work."

All the labourers were called, and they brought with them anyone who would help. By the end of the day, every stone was back on the original field.

That night, the vicar left two of the younger workmen watching over the site. Their services had been bought with a basket of bread, ham and two large bottles of beer. They were instructed not to fall asleep.

The sun had barely risen the next day as the two lads hammered at the vicarage door. The vicar pulled on his gown and ran downstairs.

"We came straight here," said the older one, "It's happened again. It's all gone."

"You mean you fell asleep?"

They glanced at each other and down at the floor.

"Ay we did. But if it was him, like you said, then it'd be easy for him to put us to sleep, wouldn't it?"

The vicar half smiled. The beer had been a bad idea.

Once again, every stone was brought back from Adam's field.

That night, two of the older labourers said they'd keep watch.

In the early hours one of them sat bolt upright and thumped the other.

"What's that?"

On top of the far wall stood the shadowy shape of a great lithe cat, the size of a stag. As they watched it moved slowly, its strong tail thrashing from side to side. The men grabbed hold of each other. The cat stopped and turned towards them, huge amber eyes catching the starlight. Then it leapt down soundlessly into the field. They froze as it gathered up one of the stones with its left paw and held it against its chest.

Then the man who had seen it first broke the other's hold and ran towards it, but instead of running away, the beast turned towards him and dropped the stone. He stopped. It's back arched, the tail flicked. It growled, then hissed as it leapt and pinned him to the ground.

The other workman jumped up and leapt over the gate. He raced down the track towards the vicarage, screaming for help.

By the time he returned with the vicar, every stone had disappeared. The field looked as though it had never been touched and his friend was gone.

There were no more attempts to bring the stones back. The church was built at Leyland. It's long gone now and the current parish church stands in its place, but people still talk about the 'cat stone', a gargoyle taken from the old church, said to be an exact likeness of the hellish creature.

THE EAGLE AND CHILD
LATHOM PARK

L ord Lathom had always wanted a son, but he never expected to find him the way he did.

An Irish Queen sat on a thick tree root in a wild forest with her twin babies in her arms. She had escaped the soldiers, but not the fairies or the eagle.

She lay back against the tree trunk and closed her eyes, exhausted. A few minutes later , the sound of bells and music woke her just in time to see her baby girl, smiling and gurgling, being carried away by a procession of fairies. As she stood up an eagle swooped down and seized her baby boy.

The eagle flew steadily on and on over the Irish Sea, the tiny infant held tight in its huge talons. When they reached Lathom Park in Lancashire, it flew to an old oak tree and gently dropped the child into its nest.

The next day Lord Lathom was walking through his park when he heard a baby's cry. He looked all around. The crying got louder. Finally he looked up and saw the infant's head thrown back over the edge of the eagle's nest.

He called his men to bring ladders. They lifted the child gently, pulling bits of twig and leaf off the shawl whilst keeping one eye out for the eagle.

"It's a boy M'Lord."

As they climbed down, Lord Lathom held out his arms and smiled.

He adopted the boy and named him Oskell of Lathom.

Years later, the family, now called Stanley, took the Eagle and Child as their heraldic crest.

THE FAIRY WELL
STAINING

T he young woman strode through the field, a baby strapped to her front and a large canvas bag over her shoulder. She stopped suddenly and knelt down next to a stone cairn by a small spring that was bubbling up through the grass. She took a pitcher out of her bag and carefully, with one arm around her child, lent forward to dip it into the clear water. When it was full, she sat back, took out a folded cloth and dipped it in. Loosening the strap that held her child, she looked down into his tiny face. His eyes searched the space between them, blinking, unable to focus, even though the infant was now six months old. As she lifted the cloth to her child's eyes, she heard the rustle of grass behind her. Twisting around, she saw, standing only about three feet away, a young handsome man dressed in green.

As she pulled her child close, he held out a small wooden box. He wasn't smiling, but his eyes were soft. She hesitated, but he nodded at the child and held it closer. She took it. Holding it in the hand around her child, she opened the lid. It held a pale green ointment. She looked up but he looked again at the child and drew his finger across his eyelid, the breath of a smile touching the corner of his lips. She looked down at her little one. When she looked back, he was gone. She scoured the field but there was no sign.

For a moment she did nothing. Then she took a tiny amount of the ointment on her little finger, tilted the infant's head back, and stopped. Slowly, she streaked the ointment across her own right eyelid, blinked a few times and looked around. All was well. Carefully, she smeared the ointment onto her child's eyes. He blinked, and looked straight at his mother with a steady gaze. She looked back and laughed, taking in those bright, shining, wide-awake eyes seeing her. Then she held him tight, jumped up and ran back across the field to share the good news.

A week later she was at Preston market when she saw the man dressed in green, his hands full of corn that he was taking from an open sack and stuffing into his pockets. The stall holder was facing the other way. She ran up to him, whispering loudly, "What do you think you're doing?"

He stopped and looked at her in amazement. Meanwhile the stall holder had turned back and was addressing her, "Who on earth are you talking to Miss?" She looked from one to the other. The man in green pointed at her right eye. She saw a white flash and he was gone, along with the sight in that eye.

It never returned, and she never saw him again.

THE LOP-EARED RABBIT
CRANK

P ullen lay in bed cursing. This damned illness had taken him by surprise and he ached all over.

In the village of Crank, there was an old woman, well known for her knowledge of herbs, who lived with her granddaughter, Jennie, and the girl's white lop-eared rabbit. Pullen had been to see her for a remedy, but he seemed to be feeling worse not better. As he lay there, he wondered if the old crone had hexed him rather than healed him. By the time he woke up the next morning, he was sure of it.

It was ten o'clock that night when Pullen and his mate Dick Piers broke into the old lady's cottage. They found her in bed. Her screaming filled the house. Jennie ran in with her rabbit under her arm, but when she saw the two men she ran down the stairs and out of the door. She raced over the moor with Dick chasing her and Pullen straggling behind. She was small and fast and they soon lost her. As Dick reached the top of the hill the white rabbit ran out in front of them. Dick kicked at it and caught its side, rolling it over and over. Pullen caught up and joined in.

The next day Jennie was found, cold and stiff, on the moor; a huge bruise on her side and a large gash on her head.

Dick was the first to see the ghost of the white rabbit. It appeared at his side as he walked home from the pub a few weeks later. He ran on, but it kept pace with him until he reached his house. The same thing happened the next night, and the night after that. People who saw him on the third day said he was jabbering, "I'm sorry, I'm so sorry."

That was the last time anyone saw him.

A month later Pullen was walking past the old woman's cottage. She'd left the village. and already the weeds were hiding the windows. The ghostly white rabbit appeared under the gate at his feet. Pullen cried out and fled back towards his home, but it kept pace with him all the way. When he reached his gate, it blocked his entrance. He ran on, with it chasing his heels, out into open country.

He was found the next day shivering and exhausted. It wasn't long afterwards that the illness came back. Pullen never recovered. Within a year, he was dead and buried in the churchyard.

THE BOGGART'S HOLE
BLACKLEY, MANCHESTER

I t was the farmer's son who encountered it first, and all he was doing was trying to pull on a pair of new boots. He had one hand on the bannister rail while he pushed his foot into one of the boots using a shoe horn. Then, so that he had his hands free to untie the laces on the other boot, he pushed the shoehorn into a small hole in the wooden panelling beneath the stairs. It shot straight back out and hit him on the head. He nearly toppled over and had to grab the bannister again. His mum and dad came out of the kitchen to see what was going on.

When he told them what had happened, his Dad laughed. He rolled up a piece of paper and pushed it into the hole. It jumped straight back out.

It was his mum who said quietly,

"I think it must be a boggart."

The father sneered and set to blocking up the hole but as soon as he had finished, whatever it was began banging and knocking. It didn't stop, not for a moment.

All night long the knocking didn't stop. It carried on all the next day. The next evening his Dad opened up the hole again hoping to get some sleep.

But that was only the start of it all. Over the next few months, as soon as they were all in bed, the boggart woke up. Pots, pans and cutlery clattered around the kitchen, only to stop the instant the farmer went down and opened the door and start up again the second he got back into bed. Sometimes they woke up shivering to discover that their bedclothes had been pulled off and lay in a tumbled heap down the stairs.

This went on for over six months.The farmer and his family were exhausted. One morning, sitting bleary eyed over porridge, the farmer looked up at his wife.

"It's never going to stop you know. We're going to have to leave.'

Within a month it was all sorted. Their furniture was strapped to the biggest cart and the son loaded the milk churns onto the smaller one. Just as they had finished harnessing up the horses, a neighbour passed by and shouted,

"Are you flittin'?"

A small voice piped up from inside one of the milk churns. It said,

"Ay, we're flittin'!"

NOTES AND SOURCES

KING OF THE CATS
  Harland and Wilkinson, *Lancashire Legends, pp. 12-13*
  Grice, *Folk Tales of Lancashire,* pp. 6-11

It's been difficult to pin a specific location on this Lancashire tale. Harland and Wilkinson state that it was told across south Lancashire. The motif of a cat speaking when hearing of the death of another cat and then disappearing forever is also echoed in "The King of the Cats" from Kankwood, Shropshire, and "Mally Dixon" from Durham, where it's suggested the cat is a fairy in disguise.

  Joseph Jacobs also compiled a version of "The King of the Cats" from five English variants in "More English Fairy Tales".

THE DUN COW OF PARLICK
  Harland and Wilkinson, *Lancashire Legends, pp. 16-19*
  Grice, *Folk Tales of Lancashire,* pp. 94-97

Harland and Wilkinson refer to the story of the Dun Cow in explanation of the giant 'rib bone' above the door of "Old Rib" farmhouse in Whittingham (datestone: 1616). They assert that at the time of writing it was still "about a yard in length, and several inches in thickness", and that many locals said it used to be more than twice this size. A giant cow indeed! They are also quick to point out its likeness to a whale's jawbone!

Although there are few English tales citing supernatural cows who give endless milk, the Scottish, Irish and Welsh oral traditions include numerous such tales, the cows often cited as 'fairy cattle', whose milk was never-ending, or at the very least, plentiful and rich.

ICY FINGERS
Bowker, *Goblin Tales of Lancashire,* pp. 77-82

This tale is in Bowker, where it is titled "The Pillion Lady".

In Lancashire Folklore, a Boggart can refer to a wandering ghost, often connected to an unlawful killing, in this case the victim, as inferred at the end of the tale.

There are many contemporary tales of ghosts appearing on the back seats of cars and seen by the driver in the mirror while driving. Similar stories, different mode of transport.

LADY SYBIL AND THE MILK-WHTE DOE
Roby, *Traditions of Lancashire,* Vol. 1, pp. 323-331

A lengthy version of this tale is to be found in John Roby's "Traditions of Lancashire", possibly its first printed source. Near the beginning he describes Lady Sybil:

"The proud maiden of Bernshaw, was from her youth the creature of impulse and imagination—a child of nature and romance".

Later he mentions her pact with the devil, signed with her blood and giving rise to her supernatural gifts. His version of the tale is set around the time of the famous Lancashire witch trials and much is made of her repentance, both after her marriage, and again after another meeting with the devil one year later.

I made the decision to honour her return to witchery by seeing, in Roby's initial description of her, only positive attributes, and the seeds of what she became.

THE HEADLESS WOMAN

Bowker, *Goblin Tales of Lancashire,* pp. 131-139

Bowker notes that headless spectres in the north of the county most often carry their heads under their left arm, and that headless beings are possibly linked to an old Saxon belief that if a person committed a crime and was beheaded before paying the penalty, they would be condemned to wander the earth carrying their head.

The Rev. William Thornber, in his, *"The history of Blackpool and Its Neighbourhood"*, suggested that a headless boggart was another example of the wandering ghost of a homicide or suicide.

THE JUG AND THE SIXPENCE

Bowker, *Goblin Tales of Lancashire,* pp. 129-130
Harland and Wilkinson, *Lancashire Folklore,* pp. 113
Grice, *Folk Tales of Lancashire,* pp. 1-5

This tale appears in Bowker as a first hand account by 'Old Nancy' and is called "The Silver Token".

Katherine Briggs, in *"A Dictionary of British Folk Tales"*, Part B, Volume 1, pp. 354, states that fairies leaving money for people who give them hospitality was one of the most commonly cited fairy traits in the 16th and 17th centuries.

PEG O'THE WELL

The Pictorial History of the County of Lancaster, pp. 208-210
Harland and Wilkinson, *Lancashire Folklore,* pp. 171-172

The headless statue of Peg o'the Well can be found in a field
next to a well below Waddow Hall. Her head is no longer in
existence as far as we know.

The writer of *"The Pictorial History of the County of Lancaster"*
suggests that the statue may have been a relic from the 'old reli-
gion', i.e. catholicism. This would explain why she was blamed
for everything. A perfect scapegoat.

*"If a storm struck and damaged the house, Peggy was author of
the damage. If the wind whistled or moaned through the ill fitting
doors and casements, it was "Peggy at her work," requiring to be
appeased, else some sad accident was sure to come."*

They go on to give an account of the story we have here,
resulting in the 'beheading' of the statue.

It gives the first hand account of their visit to the Waddow
Hall that includes a dialogue with one of the servant girls called
Jane, *"a neat, intelligent young woman",* who was in possession of
the head of the statue at the time. These are her words:

*" 'O, I have lately brought her out of those gloomy rooms at the
top of the house, washed her face, and she now lives in the larder.' She
uttered these last words with an arch expression of look and word,
which told us that my informant was far beyond the weakness of
ordinary superstitious fears.*

*'Pray let me see her,' we added. We were conducted into a large
bright-looking pantry, and there in truth was Peggy's head. It lay -
bearing on the neck marks of violence - with the features upward, on
a long table, shining with a purity and cleanness like the atmosphere
of the locality.*

'Does she ever plague you now?'

'No, sir; there is not a better girl in all the parish. I fear she was much slandered.'"

And so Jane takes her place here in the journey of Peg's story, as Peg's champion, in direct opposition to the views of many of her contemporaries.

SKRIKER

Bowker, *Goblin Tales of Lancashire*, pp. 27-36

These black dog stories from Lancashire and Yorkshire usually take the form of a huge shaggy black dog that portends death to either the one who sees it or someone close to them. They are also known as Barguest, Padfoot, Trash or Gytrash. However, 'black dog' folklore is extant across the whole of the British Isles under and is also found in European folklore.

It's been suggested that there may be a link between 'Barguest' and the German, 'Bahr-Geist', a funeral spirit. Another proposition is that they could be traceable to accounts of the Celtic otherworld, where dogs such as the Hounds of Annwn were believed to be messengers from the world of the dead, although these animals were often described as white with red ears.

An interesting side note is that one of the earliest mentions of Gytrash in print is in Charlotte Brontë's 'Jane Eyre' (1847), where Jane remembers the tales Bessie, her nursemaid, had told her, as Rochester's dog, Pilot, appears from under a hedge.

THE TAILOR OF CHATBURN

Roby, *Traditions of Lancashire*, Vol. 2, pp. (153-177)
"The Pictorial History of the County of Lancaster", pp. 211
Harland and Wilkinson, *Lancashire Folklore*, pp. 81-82

The tale of the Tailor of Chatburn most likely first appeared in print sometime between 1818 and 1829 in "The Kaleidoscope", a literary magazine published in Liverpool by Egerton and Smith. It ran until 1831 but Roby refers to it as his source for this story in his "Traditions of Lancashire", published in 1929. It's also mentioned in *"The Pictorial History of the County of Lancaster"*, where it says the pub's location was pointed out to them by a James Driver from where they stood in the grounds of Waddow Hall by the statue of "Peg O'the Well". It was *"just above"* the nearby Brungerly Bridge that crosses the River Ribble.

It was picked up by Harland and Wilkinson in "Lancashire Folklore" in 1867 and expanded on in their "Lancashire Legends" a few years later. They end their account by saying, *"Over the door, till lately, swung the old and quaint sign, attesting the truth of the tradition and the excellence of mine host's beer."* They cite the inn as being on the Gisburn road from Clitheroe. There was a pub called "Dule Upo' Dun" in Clitheroe that was recorded as far back as 1686. However by 1789 it had been converted into cottages which burnt down in 1828.

THE WHITE DOBBIE
Bowker, *Goblin Tales of Lancashire*, pp. 152-158

In 1878, Bardsea was within the Lancashire boundary. It wasn't until 1974 that this area became part of Cumbria.

James Bowker says that the White Dobbie and his white hare were seen, most often at night in winter storms, along the Furness coastline between Bardsea and Rampside.

His restless journeying was described by Bowker *"as though his mission was one of life and death."* Many thought his incessant wandering was a punishment for some dreadful crime.

Tales of wayfaring ghosts doomed to wander the earth for eternity have a long history both in folklore and literature, from the medieval legends of the immortal man known as the Wandering Jew, condemned to walk the earth for eternity, to the literary creation of Jacob Marley in "A Christmas Carol", doomed to wander the earth in chains. Dicken's novel was first published in 1843, and so was contemporaneous with reported sightings of the White Dobbie.

Closer to home, only a few miles from Bardsea, lies Furness Abbey, where tales of encounters with ghostly monks, in their predominantly white habits are still extant today in the contemporary folklore of the area.

BURIED TREASURE
Harland and Wilkinson, *Lancashire Legends*, pp. 55-57

A version of this tale is recounted in Harland and Wilkinson. They also report that her ghost made regular appearances for many years, both along a nearby road and in the garden. One witness described her as having a withered face and wearing a striped petticoat.

THE BLACK COCKEREL
Bowker, *Goblin Tales of Lancashire*, pp. 234-237

I have found no other reference to this tale and Bowker himself does not give a location. He says that he has never before come across a tale where the devil appears as a cockerel, but that *"In this case, however, that was insisted upon."*

THE EARTHENWARE GOOSE
Bowker, *Goblin Tales of Lancashire*, pp. 167-173
Thornber, *The History of Blackpool and Its Neighbourhood*, pp. 308-309

Bowker points out that Mag Shelton (also known as Meg) didn't go far, as she was buried in Woodplumpton. She died in 1705, her body found crushed between a barrel and a wall. Her grave can still be seen today at St. Anne's Church She was known as the "Fylde Hag". Her real name, recorded at the church, was Margary Hilton.

The Rev. W. Thornber says she constantly milked her neighbours' cows, taking the milk away in a large jug, *"walking before her in the shape of a goose"*. He also describes how she was once foiled by a maiden who sat her down by a fire and stuck a bodkin crossed with two weaver's healds (same as a heddle: the part of a loom that the warp threads pass through) *"about her person"*, which fixed her in her seat, unable to move.

It is said that she kept rising from the grave. The townsfolk buried her three times and finally she was buried face down and a granite slab placed over her to prevent further wanderings.

Flowers and jewellery are still regularly left on her grave.

THE ENCHANTED FISHERMAN

Bowker, *Goblin Tales of Lancashire,* pp. 104-119

Grice, *Folk Tales of Lancashire,* pp. 125-129

Roger's entry to fairyland is marked by the sound of a submerged bell. There are many stories of submerged bells along the Lancashire coastline, as well as further afield and it has been suggested that their origins are related to the extensive Celtic lore of drowned lands.

Katherine Briggs also notes that this story is reminiscent of tales of "The Green Land of Enchantment", said to be in the Bristol Channel. This has resonances with the 12th century legend "The Green Children of Woolpit", in which two children with a green pallor to their skin appeared, saying they had followed the sound of bells from a land of perpetual green twilight.

THE SPECTRAL CAT

Bowker, *Goblin Tales of Lancashire,* pp. 63-72

This appears in Bowker. It is an example of many tales across Britain that describe stones moved to different locations while churches being as they were being built. Bowker suggests the possibility that parishioners who preferred different locations may sometimes have moved the stones themselves and invented the demonic stories in explanation.

In the archives of The Historical Society of Lancashire & Cheshire, Vol 7 (1854 - 1855), there are the minutes of a 'Miscellaneous Meeting' on 25th January 1855. In them, under the section entitled, 'Notes on the Old Church at Leyland', Miss Ffarington explains how her father bought many of the gargoyles from the old church, sold as 'old materials' and that one of them was the 'Cat Stone' that already had this story attached to it.

THE EAGLE AND CHILD

Harland and Wilkinson, *Lancashire Legends,* pp. 20-22
Westwood and Simpson, *Lore of the Land,* pp. 400-401

The tale I have retold appears in 'Lancashire Legends', where it is cited as being printed by the Lancaster Herald in the seventh volume of the Journal of the British Archaeological Association, entitled "The Fause Fable of Lord Lathom. A Fayned Tale".

Another version is that Sir Thomas Lathom had a daughter, Isabel. He wanted a male heir but his wife was now too old to conceive. He took a mistress and when the boy she bore him was placed at the foot of a tree where an eagle had been regularly seen. He then brought his wife, unwittingly, past the tree. When she saw the child, she thought that God had sent a miracle and agreed to adopt him and make him their heir. However, on his death bed, Sir Thomas had a change of heart and left the majority of his estate to Isabel.

This may appear a more plausible version of the tale, however, Westwood and Simpson state that the Sir Thomas in this tale had a son, also called Thomas, who had a daughter called Isabel. She married Sir John Stanley. Due to the deaths of the other heirs, when her father died in 1382, the estate passed through Isabel to the Stanley's.

THE FAIRY WELL

Thornber, *The History of Blackpool and Its Neighbourhood*, pp. 333-334

Harland and Wilkinson, *Lancashire Folklore*, pp.112

Thornber locates the tale in one of *"the fairies favourite spots"*: by a cold spring of water called the "Fairies' Well" between Hardhorn and Staining. This version is referred to by Harland and Wilkinson.

The Northern Aquarian, on their website, have located the only spring between Hardhorn and Staining in 1891, which is known as Wrangdom Well.

Katherine Brigg's points out in "The Dictionary of Fairies" that fairy ointment can allow the user to see through 'glamours' that fairies can lay over things, to see what's really there. It also allows the user to see through spells of invisibility.

This story also links to many "Fairy Midwife" tales that are found across Europe, and are particularly prevalent in Celtic folklore.

THE LOP-EARED RABBIT
Westwood and Simpson, *The Lore of the Land,* pp. 395-396
Whitaker, *Lancashire's Ghosts and Legends,*

Source: Westwood and Simpson. Their reference is Terence Whitaker's *"Lancashire's Ghosts and Legends"* (1980) but Whitaker doesn't share details of his informants. It doesn't appear to be mentioned in any previous publications. This story is well represented currently on the web.

However, there is a tale called "The White Hare" that has similarities to this Lancashire tale. It appears in Robert Hunt's, *"Popular Romances of the West of England"*, which was published in 1903. In it, a wronged dairymaid is found guilty of murdering her newborn child and is executed. The father of the child, whose family had succeeded in ending their relationship, turned to drink. From then on he was haunted by a white hare that constantly ran under his horse's hooves terrifying the animal. It's said that many people witnessed this apparition and that eventually the terrified horse threw him into an unused mine, where he drowned.

THE BOGGART'S HOLE
Roby, *Traditions of Lancashire,* Vol. 1, pp. 416-419
"The Pictorial History of the County of Lancaster", pp.161-162

Boggart Hole Clough, the location of the story, still appears with this name on the Ordnance Survey map in Blackley, just north east of Manchester.

It first appeared in print in 1829 in John Roby's, "Traditions of Lancashire". Roby states that he heard this tale from Irish folklorist, Crofton Croker, who had heard it from 'a very worthy old lady' who knew the place. However, Westwood and Simpson suggest that it may have been adapted by Roby from a

Yorkshire legend, "Obtrusch Roque", or an Irish tale published by Croker in the same year.

In *"The Pictorial History of the County of Lancaster"* (1844) a boy near the site was asked if he had seen the boggart, to which he replied, "There's noa Boggart neaw".

BIBLIOGRAPHY

1844. *The Pictorial History of the County of Lancaster*, London: George Routledge

Bowker, James 1878. *Goblin Tales of Lancashire*, London: W. Swan Sonnenschein & Co.

Briggs, Katharine M. 1970. *A Dictionary of British Folk-Tales*, London: Routledge & Kegan Paul

Briggs, Katharine 1977. *A Dictionary of Fairies*, Harmondsworth, Essex: Penguin

Grice, Frederick 1953. *Folk Tales of Lancashire*, London and Edinburgh: Thomas Nelson and Sons Ltd.

Harland, John and Wilkinson, T.T. 1867. *Lancashire Folk-Lore*, London: Frederick Warne and Co.

Harland, John and Wilkinson T.T. 1873. *Lancashire Legends, Traditions, Pageants, Sports & Customs*, London: G. Routledge.

Hunt, Robert 1908. *Popular Romances of the West of England*, London: Chatto & Windus

Jacobs, Joseph 1894. *More English Fairy Tales*, London: David Nutt

Roby, John 1829. *The Traditions of Lancashire, Fifth edition (1872)*, George Routledge & Sons

Thornber, Rev. William 1837. *The History of Blackpool and Its Neighbourhood*, Republished by The Blackpool and Fylde Historical Society 1985

Westwood, Jennifer and Simpson, Jacqueline 2005. *The Lore of the Land*, London: Penguin

Whitaker, Terence W. 1980. *Lancashire's Ghosts and Legends*, London: Robert Hale Ltd.

ACKNOWLEDGMENTS

These are the people without whom this book would have been very different. Thank you to Marjan Wouda for always being an extraordinary, brilliant artist and collaborator; Janet Guild for sharp, honest and thoughtful editing and many conversations; Sue Brittain for her painstaking proof-reading and kindness; Deborah Swift for giving her time, care and patience to help me navigate technical waters; Litfest in Lancaster for supporting this leap from stage to print, and the staff of Lancashire Libraries for being incredibly helpful.

Thank you also to Professor Gary West and Dr Anja Gunderloch of the School of Scottish Studies at The University of Edinburgh, where I had the incredible good fortune to experience both their expertise and their humanity as I undertook a research Masters that irrevocably influenced my working practice and laid the ground for an ongoing enquiry into storytelling and life.

Not forgetting Sam and Sal who have always been part of the journey, and my husband, Geoff for constant support, help, and ensuring our lives continue to function, even as chaos threatens and deadlines loom.

Finally, thank you to all the tellers and listeners of these tales that have gone before, and those yet to come, without whom these stories would not be.

Jacqueline Harris
Lancaster 2025

ABOUT THE AUTHOR

Jacqueline Harris is a writer, storyteller and theatre maker, exploring the places where story, people and landscape meet. She has a Masters from The University of Edinburgh, where she undertook research into how stories are passed on.

She often collaborates with artists, film-makers and musicians to experiment with new ways of doing this through different forms, from performances and print to exhibitions and installations.

She also runs 'Storywheel' workshops: interactive storytelling, exploring how story and life talk to each other.

Find out more about Jacqueline here:

www.storywheel.co.uk

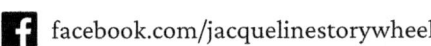 facebook.com/jacquelinestorywheel

ABOUT THE ARTIST

Marjan Wouda is a Dutch-born, Lancashire-based sculptor and artist of international standing. Her work often starts with a story. While usually featuring animals, she is passionate about exploring the human predicament in a way that is thought-provoking. She loves the adventure of the making process, exploring materials playfully and allowing them their voice. Her public sculptures can be found across the UK and further afield.

"Dandy", a great black dog, and the imposing "Sir Hare", have their origins in the stories and landscape of Lancashire.

Find out more about Marjan here:
www.marjanwouda.com

instagram.com/marjanwoudasculpture

Printed in Dunstable, United Kingdom